Manufactured in China.

8 7 6 5 4 3 2 1

ISBN 0-7853-2547-6

Pinky Piglet

Written by Catherine McCafferty

Illustrated by Lyn Martin

Publications International, Ltd.

Pinky was tired of sharing a mud puddle. No matter which way he turned, he bumped into another piglet.

So Pinky went off to make his own mud puddle. He dug a cool new spot right next to the stream. It was the perfect place for a piglet.

Pinky splashed some mud, but no one was there to splash him back. Pinky decided to let his best friend play with him, but only his best friend, no one else.

Pinky and his friend had lots of fun splashing. Then Pinky said, "Let's play pig-in-the-middle!"

They couldn't play pig-in-the-middle with only two pigs, so Pinky thought it would be okay for another friend to join them.

Before long Pinky had a great idea. "Pig pile!" he shouted. But pig piles aren't much fun with only three pigs.

Pinky asked the other piglets to join him in his new mud puddle. They made the muddiest, splashiest pig pile ever!

Now Pinky's puddle was perfect.
"Sharing is more fun than I thought,"
said Pinky. He never wanted his own
puddle again.